W9-BWR-251

THE NINE CRYING DOLLS

A STORYCRAFT BOOK

Storycraft Books are specially designed to give young people an authentic introduction to the cultural traditions of other children around the world.

THE NINE CRYING DOLLS

A Story from POLAND Retold by Anne Pellowski

Illustrated by Charles Mikolaycak

Philomel Books in cooperation with the U.S. Committee for UNICEF

Published by Philomel Books, The Putnam Publishing Group
200 Madison Avenue, New York, N.Y. 10016

This story is well-known in Poland. The version in this book has been freely translated and adapted by Anne Pellowski from Dziewiéc Placzek-nieboraczek. Lwów, 1930, by Janina Porazinska.

Library of Congress Cataloging in Publication Data

Pellowski, Anne.
The nine crying dolls.

SUMMARY: In an effort to cure her own baby of his incessant crying, a mother inadvertently starts an epidemic of crying babies in her village.
[1. Crying—Fiction. 2. Folklore—Poland] I. Mikolaycak, Charles. II. United States Committee for UNICEF. III. Title.
PZ8.1.P37Ni 1980 398.2'7'09438 [E] 79-25975
ISBN 0-399-20752-X (TB)
ISBN 0-399061162-2 (GB)

Dedicated to the memory of my paternal great-grandparents, Frank and Anna Pellowski.

NCE UPON A TIME, IN A PLACE FAR away from here there stood a poor little cottage. In the cottage lived Tatuś Bartosz and Mama Bartosz and their little baby son, Antolek. Baby Antolek cried a lot, and for no reason at all. Sometimes he started in at dawn and kept it up all day, not even stopping to eat or sleep. His mother was afraid he would cry himself to pieces. She was at her wit's end wondering what to do.

One day when Antolek was screaming at the top of his lungs, an old babka, or grandmother, came walking over the fields to the Bartosz house. She was half in rags but still, when she rapped at the door, Mama Bartosz let her in and gave her a seat by the table. Then she set a bowl of milk and bread out for the babka, for it was plain to be seen that she was hungry.

Now all this time Antolek was howling and crying, so his mother asked the old woman,

"Babka dear, do you know anything that will stop my Antolek from crying?"

The old grandmother scraped the last crumb from her bowl and then said,

"I have traveled far and near and seen many things, so you may be sure that I have

an answer for almost everything. Now, if the crying does not stop, you must cut the sleeves from some old blouses or shirts and from them make nine rag dolls. Be sure there are nine of them. Then go to the market and, when no one is looking, throw them, one by one, into the wagons and carts as they go by. That will carry the crying away."

As soon as the old babka had left, Mama Bartosz hurried up to the attic, where she found some old blouses and shirts. From the sleeves she cut out pieces for nine rag dolls. All day she cut and sewed until finally she had finished the nine dolls.

The first doll was as thin as a stick.

The second doll had a frown on her forehead.

The third doll had one eye sewn shut.

The fourth doll had a twisted nose.

The fifth doll had a patch on its cheek.

The sixth doll had her mouth turned upside down.

The seventh doll had a chin as sharp as a needle.

The eighth doll had a wrinkled neck, and the ninth doll had a hole in its head! And all of the dolls looked as if they were crying.

The next day when Mama Bartosz drove to market with her husband, she carried the dolls in a basket, covered up with a napkin. When they got to the market square, it was crowded. The first wagon to go by belonged to the baker. Into it, Mama Bartosz dropped the first rag doll, the one as thin as a stick. Then along came the carpenter, and into his cart Mama Bartosz dropped the second rag doll, the one with the frown on her forehead. The third to come by was the shoemaker, and Mama Bartosz dropped the third rag doll, the one that had one eye sewn shut, into his bag.

Then came the policeman, the blacksmith, the potter, and three farmers, and into each wagon or bag or cart Mama Bartosz secretly threw a sad-faced rag doll. That evening, when the baker got home, his baby girl began to cry and howl. When the carpenter got home, his little boy began to shriek and yammer. When the shoemaker carried his bag into his house, his baby twins began to screech and wail. In fact, in all of the nine houses where the rag dolls were brought home that evening, the children began to cry at the same time, just as if a bandmaster had lifted his baton and ordered them to start the music.

The mothers tried to quiet their babies, but the little ones only cried all the louder. They cried all night and all day. They would probably still be crying if the little old babka hadn't come walking by while the nine mothers were at the baker's house discussing what they could do to quiet their babies. When they saw the babka, they invited her to come in and, after giving her something to eat, they asked for her help. The old grandmother listened first with her left ear, then with her right ear. She could not hear very well.

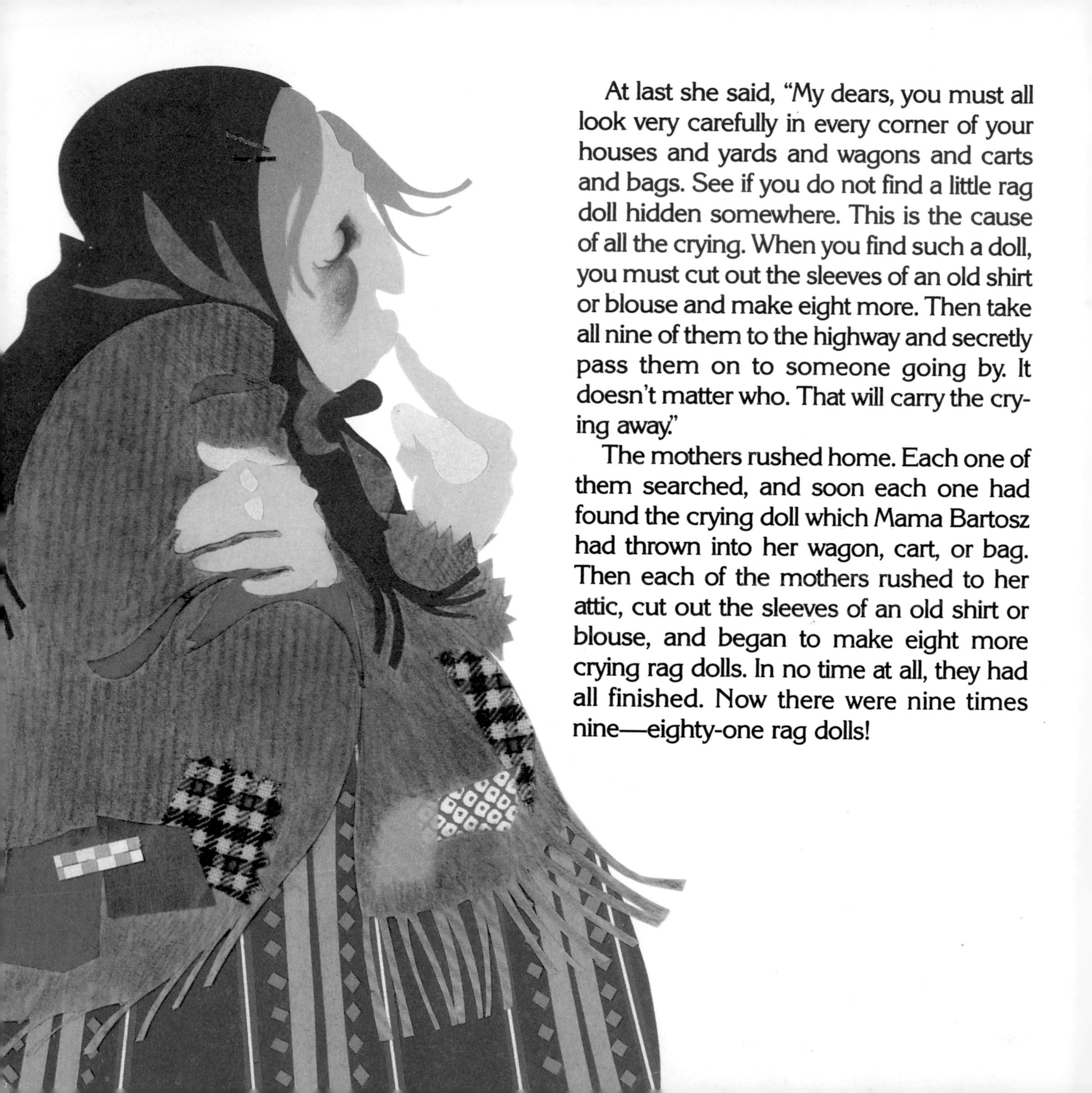

At last she said, "My dears, you must all look very carefully in every corner of your houses and yards and wagons and carts and bags. See if you do not find a little rag doll hidden somewhere. This is the cause of all the crying. When you find such a doll, you must cut out the sleeves of an old shirt or blouse and make eight more. Then take all nine of them to the highway and secretly pass them on to someone going by. It doesn't matter who. That will carry the crying away."

The mothers rushed home. Each one of them searched, and soon each one had found the crying doll which Mama Bartosz had thrown into her wagon, cart, or bag. Then each of the mothers rushed to her attic, cut out the sleeves of an old shirt or blouse, and began to make eight more crying rag dolls. In no time at all, they had all finished. Now there were nine times nine—eighty-one rag dolls!

The next day was a Sunday, and it was a special feast day, so that everyone around was sure to go to town. The mothers took all their dolls to the highway, and, one by one, they threw them into the wagons and carts and bags of the people who passed by. Tatuś and Mama Bartosz also drove by in their cart, but they did not notice as each of the nine mothers threw a doll their way. One by one, without a sound, nine little rag dolls landed softly in the basket in the back of the Bartosz's cart.

That night, when they got home, baby Antolek began to cry.

"What on earth is the matter?" asked his mother. "You have been so good for the last few days." Mama Bartosz kissed him and sang to him, but baby Antolek only cried all the louder. Finally, she reached into her basket to get him a cookie.

But oh, heavens! There in the basket lay the nine crying rag dolls!

The thin one;

the one with a frown on her forehead;

the one with one eye sewn shut;

the one with a twisted nose;

the one with a patch on its cheek;

the one with her mouth turned upside down;

the one with a chin as sharp as a needle;

the one with a wrinkled neck, and

the one with a hole in its head!

"Oh, dear," cried Mama Bartosz. "I have brought back my own crying dolls. I wanted to pass on my troubles and now they have come back to me."

Just at that moment, along came the old grandmother again.

"Well," asked the old woman, "how are things going now?"

"Babka dear, I did just as you told me, but I see that I have only passed my troubles on to hurt others, and that is something I do not want to do."

"Don't worry," said the old babka. "Take the nine crying dolls to the river. Throw them out into it and let them float far, far away from here and from anyone."

So Mama Bartosz took the nine crying dolls and threw them into the swift current, and immediately they were carried out of sight.

When she got back to the house, Antolek was jumping for joy and, as far as I know, he is still laughing happily.

As for the old babka, I think she is still busy, helping to get rid of all those other crying dolls!